PRESIDENTIAL CONVERSATIONS FOR KIDS

George S. Corey

Art by CLEO

C:NERGISTIK

NEW YORK

Copyright © 2025 by George S. Corey
All rights reserved.
Printed in the United States of America

This is a work of political satire. No part of this book may be used or reproduced in any manner whatsoever without written permission except in the case of brief quotations embodied in critical articles and reviews.

Published by Cinergistik™

Cinergistik Inc.
375 Greenwich Street
New York, New York 10013
www.cinergistik.com

ISBN 978-1-7353509-7-4

*To The Artist Cleo, for her art and heart,
the inspiration for every word*

CONTENTS

Georgie and GiGi
7

George Washington
17

Abraham Lincoln
27

Theodore Roosevelt
35

Franklin Delano Roosevelt
43

John F. Kennedy
49

Lyndon Baines Johnson
55

Richard Nixon
featuring The Impeachables:
Andrew Johnson
Bill Clinton
Donald Trump
67

Jimmy Carter
77

Ronald Reagan
87

Barack Obama
93

Joe Biden
featuring Kamala Harris
101

CLEO's Skateboard Gallery
106

Afterword
117

Acknowledgements
121

About the Author
122

About the Artist
123

We're not kiddos anymore.
We're KIDS!

Georgie and GiGi

"Oooofff!" Georgie cried out, as he stuck the landing on his skateboard. The bright-red Supreme longboard with a faded blue Smurf in sunglasses stenciled on its nose was Georgie's prized possession.

Ten-year-old George—everyone called him Georgie—was now the *first* in his class to flip his board onto the rail and ride it down the front steps of the elementary school building. It was the last day of fourth grade. School was out and summer was here! So Georgie, naturally, decided to exit the school building in trailblazing style.

Georgie already had a lot of firsts under his belt. He was the first in his class to get straight A's (okay, he got a B+ in math). He was always the first kid to get picked for athletic teams (well, except for basketball; Georgie was fast but also short). He was even the first kid in his family, older brother to his twin sisters, Abigail and Dolly.

Georgie may have been destined to be No. 1 at many things because his parents (both history teachers) had named him after the first president of the United States, George Washington. Plus, they just really liked the name George.

Georgie's classmates cheered and whooped (even some of the fifth-grade kids), but Georgie played it cool. He raised two fingers in a peace sign and motioned to his BFF, GiGi.

"Let's get outta here, G," he said.

"Already by your side, G," GiGi replied.

They bumped fists and rode away on their boards.

GiGi's board was purple, and she had traced hearts all over it in different colors. She called it "Heart Art" and got a kick out of how that rhymed. Her name was Giselle; it had been passed down over multiple generations of her family, which came from the French West Indies. But everybody called her GiGi—well, everyone except Georgie.

He called her G, and she called him G. And they thought that was pretty cool.

While Georgie was a top banana at school and sports, GiGi wasn't crazy about school (except for drama club) and hated sports (except for skateboarding, which she *loved*). GiGi thought of herself as "a star in the making." And, true to that vision, usually landed a leading role in school plays. She always wore her black hair in two pom-pom buns, and after she celebrated her 10th birthday, she was allowed to wear clear lip gloss and glitter nail polish, also clear. So, for a suburban fourth-grader, GiGi had "star quality." But she still managed to be way down to earth and liked to "keep it real," as she was fond of saying.

As they glided down the sidewalk on their boards, enjoying Astro Pops, Georgie noticed a huge rip in GiGi's jeans.

"Wow!" Georgie exclaimed. "You really tore your jeans out!"

"Yah, trying to flip my board and ride it down the steps, just like you did when you made your grand exit."

"Do not try this at home, kids," joked Georgie. "Leave it to us pros!"

"Yah, whatever. I'm convinced your board's got some kind of magical voodoo power. I bet if you let me ride it, I could do *two* flips and ride it down the steps."

"No way, G!"

"Aww, come on, please?"

"No."

"S'il vous plaît?"

Georgie laughed. "Well now that you asked in French, I'll think about it."

The two G's fist-bumped.

"Oh, hey, do you want to come over for dinner tonight?" Georgie asked. "Marie's in town. And she's making kibbeh."

"*Kibbeh?!* As in my *favorite* Middle Eastern food? Oh, I am there. Then we can hit the skate park."

'Marie' was Georgie's Egyptian grandmother. Her official name was Grandma Marie, but Georgie and GiGi, who was Grandma Marie's favorite of the neighborhood kids, referred to her simply as Marie between themselves.

Grandma Marie was *cool*. Whenever she visited, she played old-school board games like Scrabble and Battleship with Georgie and his friends. A former star forward on her all-girls Catholic high school basketball team, she'd even shot hoops with the kids. And, she was an amazing cook.

Her kibbeh were football shaped meatballs made with beef, onions, pine nuts and cracked wheat. Marie deep-fried them, refusing to bake her kibbeh just to make the moms happy. And sometimes, she'd take Georgie, GiGi and their friends out for French fries and milkshakes.

Georgie and GiGi especially loved the exotic dishes she prepared. She also made a mean grilled cheese.

Georgie's parents were attending an academic symposium in Albuquerque. He knew how to spell

Albuquerque, thanks to prep for the recent interscholastic spelling bee, but still wasn't quite sure how to pronounce it. He was just stoked that his parents took the twins with them, and that he was getting to kick off summer vacay with a feast of his favorite Middle Eastern comfort food with two of his favorite people: Grandma Marie and GiGi.

"I'm glad you have a friend like GiGi," Georgie's grandmother told him. "She's nice and smart. She laughs at your jokes and makes you laugh too. That's important."

"And she likes skateboarding too!" exclaimed Georgie. "She's definitely my BFF."

"I thought *I* was your BFF!" Grandma Marie joked.

"You're *both* my BFF," Georgie replied diplomatically.

That night, at dinner, Georgie and GiGi excitedly shared their summer plans with Grandma Marie. They envisioned a summer filled with fun, adventure, a few beach trips and lots of skateboarding.

"And your summer reading list," Grandma Marie reminded them.

"Oh, yeah, that, too!" Georgie reassured his grandmother.

The two G's hung on to every word Grandma Marie said, as she served them her famous Egyptian sugar cookies and poured two glasses of cold milk for them.

"You two are growing up so fast. And in a few months you'll be starting fifth grade! You certainly aren't kiddos anymore—you're KIDS!"

Later, as they rushed to the skate park before it got dark, Georgie and GiGi agreed that Grandma Marie was right. They weren't kiddos. They were KIDS. Suddenly, it felt like summer was full of endless possibilities.

The skate park was filled with kids of all ages. There were even some teenagers, but they mostly kept to themselves with a "too cool for school" attitude.

The younger kids all wore protective gear thanks to the parents. And just to be on the safe side, there was always a parental monitor to make sure the kids were properly padded up: with wrist and shin guards, knee pads, sometimes goggles—and, of course, helmets.

The kids personalized their protective gear just like they did their boards, especially the helmets. On any given day at the skate park, one could observe a sea of vibrant colors, mohawk tufts, blinking lights and, in GiGi's case, a purple glittery globe of a helmet adorned with hearts and peace signs. There were even separate lanes for skateboarding, BMX, scooter, wheelchair and aggressive inline skating.

GiGi breezed by and did a perfect kickflip on her first try. She was fearless; Georgie loved that about her.

"Cool!" shouted Georgie.

"You think that was cool? Check this out!"

GiGi then did a heelflip—not as perfect, but still clean. She giggled, exhilarated, and bent down to tighten her shoelaces.

Georgie whizzed by on his longboard, and invited GiGi to hop on.

"Seriously?" she said.

"Yeah, take it for a spin, G," Georgie said with a smile.

Georgie stepped off and allowed his BFF to mount his longboard.

"Let's goooooooo!" he cried, as he gave her a push. Suddenly, they picked up wicked speed, and *whoosh*, launched straight into the sky.

"Woah, what's happening G?!" cried GiGi.

"I don't know G! Maybe this thing *is* magical!"

As they flew through the sky, the longboard felt like it was attached to the bottoms of their feet. Strangely, neither of them was afraid of falling. It was too exhilarating!

A freezing rainstorm began beating down, making it difficult for them to see ahead of them.

Then, *splash*, they were gently but abruptly dropped into the frigid waters of the Delaware River. It was Christmas night 1776, and none other than General George Washington was coming to their rescue.

GEORGE

GEORGE WASHINGTON
The First President, 1789-1797

George Washington

Georgie and GiGi paddled hard through the icy cold water toward a boat that was rocking violently in the waves. Georgie somehow managed to keep his beloved longboard tucked safely under his arm.

A tall man in a long blue overcoat stretched a long, strong arm out and hoisted them aboard to safety. The kids rolled over onto their sides, gasping, as rain and sleet beat down upon their faces.

"Proceed rowing, men!" the kids' savior commanded his crew.

Georgie and GiGi caught their breath and removed their helmets as trapped water gushed out.

The man eyed these strange-looking children quizzically. He then picked up the skateboard and studied the odd contraption.

"I was summoned by my country, whose voice I can never hear but with veneration and LOVE."

GEORGE WASHINGTON

Georgie's eyes widened. "It can't be," he said to himself.

"What?" asked GiGi.

"That's George Washington. Hey! You're George Washington."

The kids gazed bug-eyed at the tall man.

"That is correct, I am General George Washington. But how did you—"

"Here, check it out," said Georgie excitedly, as he unzipped a pocket in his shorts and dug out a soaking wet dollar bill. "Look!"

Washington took the bill and was visibly startled to see his own image.

"Why ... what is this? Who are you children?"

"Well, I'm George. And this is my friend GiGi. Okay, this may be hard to believe—and I'm not even sure I understand what's going on myself—but we're from the future, I guess?"

Washington laughed. "Ah, surely the sleepless nights and battle fatigue have finally gotten to me!"

"No, we're very real ... Sir," said Georgie.

"And we know a bunch of stuff about you," added GiGi.

"Such as?" said Washington, skeptical.

Georgie rattled off a barrage of facts, "Your wife's name is Martha. You live at Mount Vernon in Virginia—that was actually our third-grade field trip."

"Yah, that was fun!" piped in GiGi.

"You're the First President of the United States—but not yet. You've got years to go before *that* will happen—and I was named after you! My parents are, like, super into history."

Washington did not know what to make of these unexpected visitors, who were both now shivering. He found two blankets for them. "Here. These may help keep you warm."

Then, Washington turned his attention to his men. Overhearing their urgent discussions, Georgie and GiGi surmised that Washington was leading his flotilla of cargo boats and river ferries, carrying some 2,400 soldiers, from Pennsylvania to New Jersey, across the Delaware River, in a surprise attack against enemy forces.

"OMG, we're in the middle of the Revolutionary War!" exclaimed GiGi. "We're literally crossing the Delaware with Washington—like in the famous painting!"

"You were right, G" said Georgie. "That board *is* magic."

"Told ya, G."

"We've got to help him. It's our patriotic duty!" Georgie scurried up to Washington, and tried to speak in Colonial English. "General, how will you navigate under these conditions?" he asked. "The night crossing is made more difficult by the, uh, uncertain thickness of the ice on the river."

"That is a good question, lad—whoever you are and from wherever you hail. The fact that our journey has been made ever more arduous by these conditions will only make our attack more stealthy. I insisted that I lead this great mission, and there is no option but to succeed."

Then GiGi had an idea. She pulled out her iPhone—complete with an ultra-cool thermal imaging case—and it still worked! They weren't kidding about waterproof, she thought to herself.

GiGi breathlessly explained to Washington how she could help him safely navigate to the other shore. Washington was awestruck.

They huddled together in the bow of the boat. GiGi crouched down, turned on the infrared night scope app, and aimed it straight ahead. The shores of New Jersey were now clearly visible through the dark night and heavy rainfall. Georgie then brought up a map of the 13 colonies on *his* iPhone. The two G's compared the infrared view on one iPhone with the historical coastal map on the other, and helped guide Washington as he passed through the ice floes to reach the shores of Trenton.

"This is a miracle!" exclaimed Washington. "You both have guided our vessels true."

Upon landing, Washington had his men ready the vessels for a swift escape after the mission had been completed. In a quiet moment, GiGi asked

Washington if sneaking up on the enemy in a surprise attack is like telling a lie.

"Oh, not the cherry tree story again! The troops do love telling that tale."

Then Washington mimicked a nobleman with a hand outstretched, saying, "I *cannot* tell a lie!" This made the kids laugh.

"But to answer your question, in this instance, no, it is not lying. A stealth invasion is a military tactic that is entirely justified, especially with the future of our country at stake."

Washington continued, "Now as I take leave of you children, and in gratitude for the feat you have performed for the benefit of our young nation this evening, I remind you of the value and power of Truth. Aspire to this ideal throughout your lives. And I implore you to understand how it was only my blunt truthfulness, from the time I was a child, that gave strength to my character and resolve to my actions. In a way, it was my pursuit of Truth, in all things, that led me here tonight. And I suppose it will have also been my pursuit of Truth that led me to become, as you have foretold, the first President of this new land. So let that be a lesson to you, children. Let that be my humble gift to you."

Suddenly, the sky flashed with artillery fire. Washington's good spirits evaporated. The great general sprang into action, commanding his troops to take the shores of New Jersey just as—BOOM!

When the black smoke and debris cleared, Georgie and GiGi found themselves once again flying through the sky atop what could now only be called a truly magical skateboard.

Abraham Lincoln

As the storm clouds cleared, Georgie and GiGi were blinded by daylight and felt the altitude plummet as they descended from the sky. They dropped onto a patch of grass. It felt like a belly flop, but way harder. They lay on their tummies for a moment and caught their breaths.

Georgie and GiGi hoisted themselves up and peered around them—nothing but a gravely dirt road.

"Where are we?" asked GiGi.

"I have no idea," replied Georgie.

Just then, a horse-drawn carriage charged down the road toward them. It was the largest carriage that they had ever seen (not that they'd seen that many horse-drawn carriages).

"Wow," Georgie marveled, "that's even bigger than my Dad's Yukon!"

"Yah, that looks like it could hold eight people!"

"Plus, two dogs."

"*And* all the family's luggage—"

"*And* a baby jogger—"

"For a week at the beach!"

GiGi waved her arms in the air and flagged down the grand carriage. As the driver pulled back on the reins, the four horses slowed and came to a halt. The kids were awestruck at the majestic carriage, which was painted a shiny black and reinforced with iron joints and metal-framed doors. The bearded and black-booted coachmen wore dark-blue military-looking uniforms adorned with brass buttons. Then, the carriage door swung open, and nestled inside was a tall man in a black stovepipe hat. There was no mistaking President Abraham Lincoln's craggy face and intense eyes.

GiGi excitedly nudged Georgie and whispered beneath her breath, *"Do you know who that is?"*

"Of course I know who it is," Georgie whispered back. *"That's why these soldiers are wearing blue. They're in the Union Army. This is the Civil War."*

"Hello there, children," said the 16th president with a weathered smile.

"Thank you for stopping, uh, Mister President," said Georgie.

Lincoln observed the children, with their strange dress and the even stranger red board on wheels. What a toll this war has taken on our nation's youngsters, he thought.

"Might you both be in need of a ride?"

As the two G's excitedly climbed into the carriage, Lincoln realized how much Georgie reminded him of his own son William, whom everyone had affectionately called Willie. Willie, age eleven, had died the year before of typhoid fever. A tear welled up in the president's eye.

"Are you okay, Mister President?" asked GiGi.

"Oh, yes, my dear child. It has been a deeply challenging time for me and my family, and most important, for our country. And now, as I look to the occasion of the dedication of the Soldiers' National Cemetery in Gettysburg, where so many men perished, my soul is burdened for these United States."

Lincoln closed his grip on the crumpled envelope in his hand. "Oh, to find the words that escape me now, with which to propel this address, this Gettysburg address," he said, frustrated. He scratched at his temples with ink-stained fingers.

GiGi tugged at Georgie's T-shirt. "OMG, he's talking about *the* Gettysburg Address," she whispered.

Georgie whispered back, "This is the most important speech of his life and maybe in the history of this country, and he's trying to write it on the back of an envelope with a quill and ink!"

Just then, Georgie remembered something. He reached into one of his cargo pockets and pulled out his prized Cross pen.

"No way," said GiGi.

"*Way*," replied Georgie with a smile.

"How much stuff have you got in those pockets?" chided GiGi.

"A lot. We learned in Boy Scouts to always be prepared."

Then Georgie said, "Mister President, please, use this. My Grandma Marie gave it to me for my birthday. She always said that sharp ideas start with sharp-looking writing instruments!"

Lincoln marveled at this new contraption and proceeded to scribble on the envelope.

"Ah, wondrous!" he exclaimed.

With Georgie and GiGi sitting on either side of him, Lincoln began scratching out sentences and hurriedly rewriting, the words suddenly spilling out of him.

Four score and seven years ago

"What does score mean?" asked GiGi.

"The word score means twenty years," Lincoln replied. "So four score and seven refers to 87 years.

That is how many years have passed since the Declaration of Independence in 1776."

"Oh, you refer to the past as a way of reminding people about our history and all that America stands for!" GiGi exclaimed.

"Precisely," replied Lincoln.

Our fathers brought forth on this continent a new nation

"You mean the Founding Fathers?" asked Georgie.

"Very good, young man," replied Lincoln.

Conceived in liberty, and dedicated to the proposition that all men are created equal.

"This is to remind people that the nation was created to gain liberty, which is another word for freedom," explained Lincoln.

"Like emancipation," GiGi said. "You did the Emancipation Proclamation, too."

"Indeed," nodded Lincoln, with a warm smile. "That Proclamation stated that all persons held as slaves within any State, or designated part of a State, shall be free!"

Now we are engaged in a great civil war, testing whether that nation, or any nation so conceived, and so dedicated, can long endure. We are met on a great battlefield of that war.

President Lincoln closed his eyes for a moment and said, "The great battlefield is the Battle of Gettysburg where the losses totaled tens of thousands of human lives. And yet, it was only one battle."

> *We come to dedicate a portion of it, as a final resting place for those who died here, that the nation might live. This we may, in all propriety do.*

"You're talking about all the people who sacrificed their lives for the benefit of everyone else, and how that should inspire us, right?" asked Georgie.

"And how honoring them is the right thing to do," added GiGi.

"That is correct, children," Lincoln replied.

> *But, in a larger sense, we cannot dedicate, we cannot consecrate, we cannot hallow this ground. The brave men, living and dead, who struggled here, have hallowed it, far above our poor power to add or detract.*

Georgie blurted out, "Oh! You're saying that words can't even come close to what the brave soldiers who actually fought for freedom did."

"I seriously have chills, this is so good!" exclaimed GiGi, quietly clapping her hands.

> *The world will little note, nor long remember what we say here; while it can never forget what they did here.*

"I am using these words to move from the present to the future—so that the soldiers who lost their lives shall not be forgotten," Lincoln said quietly.

It is rather for us, the living. We here be dedicated to the great task remaining before us

"Now you're telling people that it's not over yet," said Georgie.

"Yah, there's *way more* to be done," added GiGi, giving President Lincoln an assuring pat on his shoulder. "But don't worry, it will all work out—you'll see."

That, from these honored dead we take increased devotion to that cause for which they here, gave the last full measure of devotion that we here highly resolve these dead shall not have died in vain;

"Those we lost did not die without reason," Lincoln said to himself. "And we must honor them by continuing to fight for what is right and just."

That the nation, shall have a new birth of freedom, and that government of the people, by the people, for the people, shall not perish from the earth.

"Thank you, children," said President Lincoln, turning to Georgie and GiGi. "I do not quite know how, but you helped me find the words."

Then he held up Georgie's Cross pen. "And I am keeping this!"

Suddenly, Lincoln and his carriage vanished into thin air.

Theodore Roosevelt

Georgie and GiGi were spun into a cloud of dust as a team of horses stampeded past them. It was now July 1, 1898 and the two G's had found themselves in the middle of the Spanish-American War.

Suddenly, none other than Colonel Teddy Roosevelt scooped them up by the scruffs of their T-shirts and pulled them atop his horse.

"Hang on, children!" he shouted boisterously. Roosevelt led his Rough Riders (the name given to the brave First U.S. Volunteer Cavalry that became famous under his leadership) as they charged San Juan Hill in Cuba.

Georgie hung on tight to Teddy, as GiGi hung on to Georgie, the skateboard wedged between them as they galloped through the dust cloud. It felt as if they were in a cartoon or old Western movie come to life. The two G's squinted, barely able to see anything through the dust.

As the dust cleared, Teddy's horse slowed to a canter, then to a leisurely trot. They were now in the middle of a beautiful desert landscape. There was nothing but nature and an endless sky. Everything looked different.

Roosevelt also looked different from the dust-covered cowboy who had rescued them. He was wearing a flannel shirt, jodhpurs, and spit-shined boots, and he had a bandana tied around his neck.

"Welcome to the year 1906, and to the Petrified Forest, children," Roosevelt announced. "But don't be scared, despite the name."

"How'd we get here? And how is it suddenly 1906?" asked Georgie.

"Do you think you children and *that thing* (he pointed to the skateboard in Georgie's arm) are the only ones touched by magic?" He continued, "We are in the middle of one of five national parks—this one in the great state of Arizona—that I have established as President of these magnificent United States."

"Oh, yah!" exclaimed GiGi. "We learned about that in school. You're 'the conversation president!'"

Roosevelt corrected her with a smile. "Con-ser-vation, young lady, meaning the protection of our precious natural resources—including the establishment of 150 national forests, 51 federal bird reserves, 18 national monuments, four national game reserves, and, as I said, five national parks. All of this for the benefit of future generations—like yours. So, if one of my legacies is that of a great environmentalist, it will bring me great satisfaction."

GiGi nodded along to Roosevelt's words, saying "My Mom is an environmentalist, too."

"She is?" asked Georgie.

"Didn't you ever see the bumper sticker on the back of her Prius? It has a picture of our planet and reads in big letters LOVE YOUR MOTHER. Get it? *Mother Earth*."

"Oh, cool!" exclaimed Georgie.

"Yes, wonderful!" chimed in Roosevelt.

"What made you fall in love with nature?" Georgie asked the president.

"Ah, well, as a boy, I was small and weak, and often the target of bullies. I suffered from a severe, rather debilitating case of asthma, you see. But my father, bless him, put me on a vigorous exercise program, from mountain climbing to boxing to wrestling. And I soon discovered that physically exerting myself actually lessened my asthma. So I grew to love physical activity and the great outdoors. And, it must be said, as I became stronger,

"The lack of power to take joy in outdoor nature is as real a misfortune as the lack of power to take JOY in books."

THEODORE ROOSEVELT

in both mind and body, the bullies didn't bother with taunting me anymore."

"Oh, we're totally against bullying," Georgie assured the 26th president.

"We are one thousand percent anti-bullying," added GiGi dramatically.

"Good!" said Roosevelt, pleased. "As the saying goes, often attributed to yours truly, speak softly and carry a big stick."

"What does that mean?" asked Georgie.

"Well, interpretations may vary, but for you children, suffice it to say *be nice*. People will respect you for it and admire your quiet strength."

"Hey, can I ask you something?" said GiGi. "Before I was a *kid*, back when I was just a *kiddo*, I had this really cute stuffed toy bear, and my parents said that it was called a 'teddy bear' named after you. Is that true?"

"Yes, it is!" chuckled Roosevelt. "That honor came from my refusing to shoot a young bear while on a hunting expedition. Word of that story spread and the term 'teddy bear' was born."

Georgie nudged GiGi excitedly, "Hey, G, have you ever gone skateboarding in a national park?!"

"No! Have you?"

"Nope. Do you want to?"

"Sure!"

As Georgie and GiGi balanced themselves on the longboard, Teddy Roosevelt gave them a soft push and propelled them into the year 1941, where they would soon meet Teddy's fifth cousin, the "other President Roosevelt": FDR.

Franklin Delano Roosevelt

Georgie and GiGi rolled down a busy street in Washington, D.C. Everything was now in black and white, like an old movie.

A motorcade was making its way down the avenue. "Check it out, G," Georgie said. "They made cars the size of *school buses* back then!"

Inside a big, old-timey convertible, a man's gloved hands held a newspaper in front of his face. The two G's squinted to make out the date on the paper's front page: December 6, 1941. Then, the newspaper dropped to reveal Franklin Delano Roosevelt, the 32nd president of the United States.

"Look, it's FDR, the president we just learned about in school!" exclaimed GiGi. "And he's riding in the Sunshine Special! Remember, that's the nickname everybody called his tricked-out presidential convertible."

"Yeah, and do you remember what tomorrow is?"

"Oh no," said GiGi, trembling, "*December 7, 1941*. The attack on Pearl Harbor. That's what led the United States into World War II. OMG, what are we going to do?"

"The only thing we have to fear is fear itself," declared Georgie, repeating FDR's famous line from his first inaugural address. "We have to be fearless, just like FDR. Come on, we've got to warn him!"

As the Sunshine Special rode past them, Georgie and GiGi tried to catch up. But they never got the chance to warn FDR.

Just as they were picking up speed, they jumped time and space and suddenly found themselves in the most famous room in the White House: the Oval Office. It was one day later: December 7, 1941.

———

Georgie and GiGi were alone. Everything around them still looked like it was in a black-and-white movie. It reminded them of *The Wizard of Oz*, how the movie started in black and white. They remembered watching it with Marie, huddled together on the couch under a big blanket.

Georgie still had nightmares about the Wicked Witch of the West and her flying monkeys. GiGi, on the other hand, delighted in every minute of the movie. She imagined herself playing Dorothy on stage, clicking her ruby slippers together and singing *Over the Rainbow* under a spotlight.

A small dog scurried up to them from out of nowhere. GiGi scooped him up into her arms and kissed the top of his head. "We're definitely not in Kansas anymore."

"And that's definitely not Toto," said Georgie.

FDR's Scottish terrier Fala jumped out of GiGi's arms and led the children down a ramp. The ramp had been built to accommodate the president's wheelchair, which he used occasionally on account of having polio.

Fala led the way, and the two G's followed on the skateboard. The sturdy ramp made for a seamless trip to President Roosevelt's study.

The mood in the room, lined with important-looking people, many dressed in military uniforms, was very serious. No one even noticed as Georgie, Gigi and Fala quietly entered.

President Roosevelt had just been told about the bombing of Pearl Harbor. His New Deal was leading America out of its greatest economic danger yet, the Great Depression. Now there was an even greater danger. America had been attacked by Japan. And four days later, Nazi Germany, led by Adolf Hitler, would declare war on America.

"I'm going before Congress tomorrow," Roosevelt said. "Time to write a speech."

His secretary Grace Tully took notes as Roosevelt began to speak. He chose his words and even punctuation marks very carefully.

Roosevelt began, "Yesterday – *comma* – December 7th – *comma* – 1941 – *dash* – a date which will live in infamy...."

"Hey G," GiGi whispered, as she nudged Georgie. "I feel so bad. I want to tell him that everything's gonna be okay, that we're gonna win the war."

"Okay," Georgie whispered back. "But let's not interrupt him. Let him finish writing his speech first."

As thrilling as this adventure was, GiGi, like Dorothy, yearned for home. She kicked the heels of her sneakers together, not thinking anything of it. And in a flash, the two G's were at Georgie's house, sitting on the couch in the TV room.

John F. Kennedy

It was completely dark except for color bars illuminating the television screen.

"Wait, did that just happen?" asked Georgie.

"Yah," GiGi nodded. "Unless we both had the *exact* same dream at the *exact* same time, which isn't likely. Look!"

GiGi pointed to the red longboard, which was now on the floor directly in front of the TV. They stood up from the couch and slowly approached the magic skateboard. As they got closer, the color bars started getting wavy, as a familiar voice was transmitted through the television's speakers.

And so, my fellow Americans: ask not what your country can do for you—ask what you can do for your country.

Georgie and GiGi looked at each other.

"I think we're about to meet JFK," Georgie said. "Marie told me he was 'the first television president.' TV was still new back then, and he aced it."

As if on cue, Georgie and GiGi reached down and touched the skateboard. Suddenly, the screen turned bright blue. Then, it spoke to them. "Don't be afraid, children. Come on, dive in. The water is fine."

The screen then enveloped them like an ocean wave. And, suddenly, they were atop the longboard, skidding to a stop on a flagstone path on White House grounds.

"Whooah, take it easy there," a man's voice said in a thick New England accent.

And there was President John F. Kennedy, with his children, John-John, age two, and Caroline, age five.

"There's no skateboarding at the White House," the 35th president told them with a wink.

"Finally!" exclaimed George. "A president who knows what a skateboard is!"

President Kennedy and his children were feeding carrots and apples to a pony right on the White House lawn.

"Oh, he's adorable!" said Gigi, petting the pony. "What's his name?"

"Macaroni!" little Caroline cried out. "He's mine!"

Kennedy invited the two G's to sit with him on the terrace, as the Kennedy children were led inside by their nanny. Georgie and GiGi noticed the president walking stiffly and holding onto his back, as if in pain.

"I'm always impressed by the vigor (he pronounced it *viguh*) of American young people," JFK said, smiling. "I may be the youngest person ever elected president, but I certainly don't feel it sometimes."

"Why not?" asked GiGi.

"Oh, just a war injury."

Kennedy recounted that during World War II in the South Pacific, he had captained an 80-foot torpedo boat called PT-109. A Japanese destroyer sliced through it, splitting the boat in two. Kennedy and his surviving crew members held onto the remains of the boat for 11 hours, hoping to be rescued. When no one came to help, he decided that they had to swim to the nearest island, which was three miles away. It took them *four hours*.

After being stranded on the island for many days, Kennedy had the idea to scratch out a message on a coconut: "11 ALIVE...NEED SMALL BOAT...KENNEDY." He sent the coconut off with island natives, and JFK and his men were rescued soon after.

He returned home a war hero, then became a congressman and eventually a senator from Massachusetts. And then, he became president.

"And you wrote the famous book *Profiles in Courage*! I read it!" exclaimed Georgie. "Well, the Young Readers Edition. I even got an A on my book report."

"And you started the Peace Corps!" added GiGi. Then, as if reciting something she'd memorized: "The Peace Corps is a program of the United States that trains and deploys volunteers—nurses, teachers, construction workers—to help people all around the world."

Kennedy marveled at his young visitors, "You children certainly are well-informed."

"Yah, we have a *really good* history teacher," GiGi said.

"She rules," added George.

"May I run something by you?" JFK asked, as he flipped through a stack of papers. "I'm working on a speech I'm set to give at the American University in a few hours. And I find young people's minds to be the most open, and young people themselves to be most direct in their feedback."

"Cool beans!" said Georgie.

"What is your speech about?" asked GiGi.

"It's about…peace. I want to be known as the president who made peace with our arch-enemy the

Soviet Union. While I will keep our United States military strong, I will do everything in my power to avoid war. Here's the passage I want to run by you":

> *In the final analysis, our most basic common link is that we all inhabit this small planet. We all breathe the same air. We all cherish our children's future. And we are all mortal.*

The president looked up to see his young audience's reaction. Georgie and GiGi nodded and smiled. JFK continued:

> *The United States, as the world knows, will never start a war. We do not want a war. We do not now expect a war. This generation of Americans has already had enough—more than enough—of war and hate and oppression.*

> *We shall be prepared if others wish it. We shall be alert to try to stop it. But we shall also do our part to build a world of peace where the weak are safe and the strong are just.*

After a moment, the kids started applauding. This made the president chuckle. They spent the rest of the afternoon talking and laughing.

Neither Georgie nor GiGi had the heart to tell their newfound friend about the fate he would meet just a few months later on a November day in Dallas.

Lyndon Baines Johnson

Georgie and GiGi found themselves back in the present day, standing outside Apparition Skateboards, a store in Austin, Texas.

GiGi looked up and read the street sign with an exaggerated Texan twang, "Guadalupe Street." An expert mimic who quickly picked up accents of all kinds, GiGi learned her South Texas accent from her next-door neighbor, Mrs. Mariette, who hailed from San Antonio.

"It's the first time on this adventure that everybody is dressed like us!" said Georgie. "And look, a 7-Eleven! Score!"

"Oh, I know," said GiGi excitedly. "Let's check out this super cool-looking skate shop, then go get Slurpees!"

"Not so fast now," a voice said. Out of nowhere, President Lyndon Baines Johnson, otherwise known as LBJ, appeared and introduced himself. "Howdy, young people!"

The two G's gazed up at the tall Texan in a 10-gallon hat.

"Y'all were taking long enough to get to me, and I ain't a patient man," the 36th president told them. "Now, I don't have a magical skateboard, but I do have a train that some folks say is magic. It's called the Lady Bird Special."

"What's a Lady Bird Special?" asked Georgie. "It sounds like something on a diner menu."

"Nooooo siree," said Johnson. "Lady Bird is my wife, the finest first lady in history, I'd say."

"What kind of name is Lady Bird?" asked GiGi.

"Her given name is Claudia, but everybody calls her Lady Bird, and it suits her just fine," replied LBJ. "Now, how about we skedaddle out of this skateboard situation. We've got a train to catch."

"A *magic* train," Georgie added.

"What makes it magical, Mr. LBJ—I mean, Mr. President?" asked GiGi.

"Y'all will see," Johnson replied with a smile.

And just like that, the two G's and LBJ were aboard the Lady Bird Special—the 19-car train that had carried Lady Bird Johnson on a four-day whistle-stop tour on behalf of her husband's presidential campaign in 1964.

As the train chugged along, Georgie and GiGi gazed out the windows and marveled at the breathtaking scenery.

"Aren't those just the prettiest wildflowers and forests you could imagine, straight out of a fairytale. Why, even the frogs are mighty handsome. That's what Lady Bird made her mission when we were in the White House—the beautification of America! In fact, it was called the Beautification Project."

"Aw, your wife sounds amazing," said GiGi. "I wish we could meet her, too."

"Say no more, children," said Lady Bird, suddenly appearing with a brown bag lunch in each hand. She wore a sheath dress with matching jacket, and her dark hair was styled in a retro bouffant. She was soft-spoken and had kind eyes. As she handed Georgie and GiGi the lunch bags, she said, "Now, children, you all are old enough to appreciate what I'm about to tell you. Every living person and thing responds to beauty. Whenever you face challenges, I want you to remember all the beauty this country holds. And I hope you are as inspired by it as I have been.

"For me, wildflowers are joy-giving."
Lady Bird Johnson

"Where flowers bloom, so does hope."
Lady Bird Johnson

"You may read these words of mine in one of your schoolbooks. And I can assure you they are just as true, if not more true, today":

Though the word beautification makes the concept sound merely cosmetic, it involves much more: clean water, clean air, clean roadsides, safe waste disposal and preservation of valued old landmarks as well as great parks and wilderness areas.

Georgie and GiGi loved hanging out with Lady Bird. She was smart, kind, told great stories—and had a very cool nickname.

After an unforgettable train tour with LBJ and Lady Bird as their guides, they were back in Austin, where the doors of the LBJ Presidential Library were opened to them.

"Wow," GiGi marveled. "I've been to libraries before, but I've never been to a presidential library."

"There must be a lot of books in here," Georgie said.

"Not just books. My papers, too. You can watch my speeches. And uh, I taped many of the conversations I had during my presidency. No other president can offer that to you—not even Nixon, who I'm sure you'll encounter soon enough. And you can listen to 'em all right here."

"It's like eavesdropping on history. But because it's a library, it's okay!" exclaimed Georgie.

"Now y'all hunker down like jackrabbits in a dust storm," LBJ told them. "You've got some serious learning to do. Go on now."

The two G's spent the rest of the day unleashed in this presidential playground.

The first thing they did was watch LBJ's famous "We Shall Overcome" speech before Congress. It was from 1965 and in black and white, but the president's words were as colorful as Lady Bird's wildflowers.

> ….*My first job after college was as a teacher in Cotulla, Texas, in a small Mexican-American school. Few of them could speak English, and I couldn't speak much Spanish. My students were poor and they often came to class without breakfast, hungry. They knew even in their youth the pain of prejudice. They never seemed to know why people disliked them. But they knew it was so, because I saw it in their eyes. I often walked home late in the afternoon, after the classes were finished, wishing there was more that I could do. But all I knew was to teach them the little that I knew, hoping that it might help them against the hardships that lay ahead.*
>
> *Somehow you never forget what poverty and hatred can do when you see its scars on the hopeful face of a young child.*

...It never even occurred to me in my fondest dreams that I might have the chance to help the sons and daughters of those students and to help people like them all over this country.

...This is the richest and most powerful country which ever occupied this globe. The might of past empires is little compared to ours. But I do not want to be the president who built empires, or sought grandeur, or extended dominion.

I want to be the president who educated young children to the wonders of their world. ... I want to be the president who helped the poor to find their own way and who protected the right of every citizen to vote in every election.

I want to be the president who helped to end hatred among his fellow men and who promoted love among the people of all races and all regions and all parties.

Then they learned about all the incredible laws that were passed during LBJ's presidency. In 1964, the Civil Rights Act made discrimination on the basis of race, color, religion, sex or national origin illegal. The Voting Rights Act of 1965 prohibited racial discrimination in voting. Also in 1965, at the base of the Statue of Liberty, President Johnson signed into law the Immigration and Nationality

Act, which allowed more people from around the world to become United States citizens.

Later, Georgie and GiGi met up with LBJ to share all that they had learned. "Wow, there's so much about you we didn't know," said Georgie, beaming. "Because of you, my family was able to come to this country from Lebanon and Egypt!"

Then Georgie did something unexpected. He stood military straight, and saluted LBJ like a Marine, saying, "Thank you, Sir." He remained in that position until the president returned his salute.

GiGi then said, "And I want to thank you for helping Black people exercise their constitutional right to vote in this country. I cannot wait until I'm 18 so that I can vote!"

"I didn't realize that you actually *knew* Martin Luther King!" exclaimed Georgie.

"Neither did I! That's so cool," added GiGi.

LBJ said that while he was proud of all that he had accomplished as president, the work wasn't done. It never is, he told Georgie and GiGi, because democracy is a living thing—not just some ideal you read about in history books.

The two G's collected the longboard from the coat check (there's no skateboarding in libraries, and *definitely not* in presidential libraries), and LBJ bid them farewell with these words: "Remember this, as you make your way into the world—something I've always believed: Don't spit in the soup. We all gotta eat."

And with that, Georgie and GiGi were off, picking up speed on the magical skateboard until they were once again skimming the clouds. Their next destination on this wild adventure: the Kennedy Center for the Performing Arts, right in the nation's capital, where a song-and-dance routine like none they'd ever seen awaited them.

RICHARD NIXON
The 37th President, 1969-1974

ANDREW JOHNSON
The 17th President, 1865-1869

BILL CLINTON
The 42nd President, 1993-2001

DONALD TRUMP
The 45th President, 2017-2021

Richard Nixon
featuring The Impeachables:
Andrew Johnson
Bill Clinton
Donald Trump

Georgie and GiGi were now seated in a VIP (that stands for "Very Important Person") box inside the Kennedy Center. It was empty except for them.

The lights dimmed and the red velvet curtain lifted to reveal a stage set of the Oval Office. And Richard Nixon, the 37th president, who was forced to resign in 1974, was center stage.

Nixon was wearing something very similar to what Elvis Presley wore in 1970, when "The King of Rock and Roll" visited Nixon in the White House.

The former president looked funny wearing a velvet cape coat and humongous gold belt, but he thought it made him look less stiff.

Spotlight on Nixon

NIXON

Thank you, thank you very much. With all the dishonest politicians in Washington, I am still the *only* president who was forced to resign. Why, you ask?

The House of Representatives may impeach the president; *but*, for the president to be removed from office, the United States Senate must vote for conviction. In my case, I knew that the House was going to impeach me and that the Senate was going to convict me. So, I had no choice but to resign.

You see, in 1972, I was running for re-election—as the Republican, of course—and my campaign…well, there was a break-in of the Democratic National Committee's headquarters…and uh, I guess you could say my campaign was involved. That's a big no-no for any kids out there in the audience tonight.

So, I had to step down, as many of you know, and my vice president, Gerald Ford, took over as president. Before I left the White House, I said, "Those who hate you don't win unless you hate them, and then you destroy yourself."

But this is what I really want to say to you people tonight. And I want to say it in song.

As the hidden orchestra played, Nixon crooned a bluesy song into the microphone.

NIXON

This political game
Has brought me fame
Has brought me sha-a-a-ame
And I'll never be the same
I'm sorry Truly sorry

I couldn't be more sorry

The music suddenly turned up-tempo, as Nixon made jazz hands and kicked up his heel.

NIXON

That I got caught

Lights down

Spotlight on Andrew Johnson, the 17th president of the United States, stage right

JOHNSON

Good evening. I have the distinction of being the *first* president to be impeached by the House of Representatives. Always nice being first, I say.

And, yes, one would say I was guilty of high crimes and misdemeanors, abuses of presidential power, violating a federal statute, and so forth.

But—and it's a very important but—I was *acquitted* by the Senate. So, unlike this Nixon gentleman, while I was impeached, I was not removed from office, nor was I forced to resign.

(singing)

Impeachment is not that bad
So many other things are much more sad
When the House votes to indict
But the Senate says no, it's alright
They can no longer call me a cad

Lights down

Spotlight on Bill Clinton, the 42nd president of the United States, stage left

CLINTON

Well, hello there. Just like 'ole Andy Johnson, I, too, was impeached by the House of Representatives. And I, too, was then *acquitted* by the Senate.

They had me on perjury, which is just a fancy way of saying I lied even after I promised to tell the truth. You should never do that. Take it from George Washington—a great president, and our *first* president—tell the truth, kids. They find out in the end, anyway.

So I served out my second term, and was president for eight years, baby.

(singing)

Impeachment is not that bad
So many other things are much more sad
When the House votes to indict
But the Senate says no, it's alright
It's really...kind of rad

Lights down

Spotlight on Donald Trump, the 45th president of the United States, center stage

TRUMP

Amateurs! These guys are amateurs. I have been impeached twice. You heard that right, *twice*!

Once, in 2019, when they say I asked for help from a foreign country in my reelection bid—which I'm told you're not allowed to do. And once, in 2021, a week before I left office, for supposedly inciting an insurrection—which you're also not allowed to do.

Both times the House of Representatives voted to impeach Donald Trump. And both times, the Senate said, no, Trump can stay.

(singing)

Impeachment is not that bad
So many other things are much more sad
When the House votes to indict
But the Senate says no, it's alright
You know Trump's outta sight

Lights down

As spotlights darted around the stage, an announcer's voice squeaked through the sound system.

ANNOUNCER

You've seen them solo tonight. Now, performing together for the first time, please welcome everybody's favorite presidential singing trio, The Impeachables! With special guest Richard "Tricky Dick" Nixon!

Lights up

The grand finale. Against the backdrop of a huge American flag, Presidents Trump, Clinton and Johnson sashayed onstage perfectly in step to the music. Dressed in matching black suits, with white shirts, skinny black ties and sunglasses, they were doing their best to look as cool as the band BTS.

TRUMP, CLINTON, JOHNSON

This political game
Has brought us fame
Has brought us shame
And we'll never be the same

Now the three former presidents formed a kick line.

We're so-o-o-orry
Truly so-o-o-orry
We couldn't be more sorry

Suddenly, Nixon, also dressed as a BTS wannabe, dropped down on a bungee cord, suspended in midair above the trio.

NIXON, TRUMP, CLINTON, JOHNSON
That we-e-e-e go-o-ot cau-aught

Lights down

JIMMY

JIMMY CARTER
The 39th President, 1977-1981

Jimmy Carter

And, just like that, Georgie and GiGi were again zipping through the sky atop the magic skateboard. The clouds, grouped in many different colors, looked like tie-dye puffs.

"Hey, how did that happen?" Georgie wondered aloud.

"Just go with it," replied GiGi.

They were soon greeted by a beautiful woman who flew alongside them. She looked like a fortune teller. Fiery red hair spilled down her shoulders from beneath a gold turban, a multi-colored cape swirling around her. Purple-tinted glasses worn at the tip of her nose made her clear blue eyes visible.

"Greetings, Georgie and GiGi!"

"How do you know our names?" asked GiGi.

"I know everything," the woman said, smiling. "I even know which president you will be seeing next."

"*Which one?*" Georgie asked excitedly.

"My daddy," she replied, giggling.

As the three of them tumbled down from the tie-dye sky, Georgie and GiGi witnessed the beautiful woman transform into a young girl their age, with reddish blonde pigtails and thick glasses.

They landed on the White House lawn. Then, the young girl led them back to her tree house. A Siamese cat was circling a small table on which a pitcher of lemonade and a plate of oatmeal cookies had been set.

"Welcome to my tree house, y'all! I'm Amy Carter! President Jimmy Carter's daughter," she said, as she carefully poured from the pitcher into three Dixie cups. "Would you like some lemonade?"

"Was that you up there in the clouds? How were you able to become a kid again?" asked GiGi.

"That sure was me; just a little trick I play sometimes," said Amy. "It's my cat here, Misty Malarky Ying Yang, that does it—I'm not sure exactly how, but she does! This kitty's got some kinda special powers. Like your skateboard, I guess. I've got a dog, too. His name is Grits. But he doesn't have whatever it is that Misty Malarky Ying Yang here does. Grits is just a regular ole dog."

"So, the woman we met…is that *you* when you grow up?" GiGi asked her.

"Kinda. She's who I want to be when I grow up. Of course, last week I wanted to be a ballerina, and Misty Malarky Ying Yang had me flyin' around in a tutu. Cookie?"

As they munched on cookies and drank lemonade, Amy told Georgie and GiGi all about what it was like growing up at the White House. She turned ten years old the year her family moved in. And even though there weren't a whole lot of kids around, Misty Malarky Ying Yang sure kept things interesting.

Thanks to Misty cat's miracles, Amy was able to assume different personas and travel backward and forward through time. As she explained it, she knew pretty much everything about her father's presidency—even stuff that hadn't happened yet—so Amy thought that made her the best person to teach them about her daddy, Jimmy Carter, the 39th president of the United States.

As Amy talked, GiGi stroked Misty Malarky Ying Yang's fur and Georgie scratched the top of the cat's head.

"Listen," Amy told them. "My daddy is an honorable man, but he's also a complicated man and had a complicated presidency. It's not like he had

"My FAITH demands that I do whatever I can, wherever I am, whenever I can, for as long as I can with whatever I have to try to make a difference."

JIMMY CARTER

one great accomplishment during his one term that you can remember him by.

"On the *first* day of his presidency, he thanked his predecessor, Mr. Gerald Ford (even though Ford was a Republican and Jimmy was a Democrat) for all Ford did to heal the country after Mr. Nixon resigned. And on the *last* day of his presidency, he negotiated for the safe release of the American hostages that were being held captive over there in Iran.

"In between, Jimmy kept the peace in this country, and he helped create peace between Egypt and Israel. Many people thought that wasn't gonna be possible on account of those two countries not being so friendly with each other up to that point."

"I knew that!" Georgie cried out. "I'm Egyptian-American, so I think that's *super* cool."

"It sure is," continued Amy. "Many years later, in 2002, in recognition of his decades of work trying to find peaceful solutions to many of the world's problems, my daddy was awarded the Nobel Peace Prize—which looks like an Olympic gold medal, but you don't wear it around your neck.

"When he was president, Jimmy got Americans to conserve energy, even though many people complained about it. And because he'd been a peanut farmer, he cared a lot about the environment and helped make the air we breathe and the water we drink cleaner.

"I may be most proud, though, of what my daddy and momma accomplished after they left the White House. Goes to show you that anybody can make a difference; you don't need to be the president or first lady, or have any title at all, really.

"I am so inspired by my parents' work with Habitat for Humanity through their organization called the Jimmy & Rosalynn Carter (that's my momma, the former first lady) Work Project."

"What's Habitat for Humanity?" asked GiGi.

"They help build houses for poor people," Amy told them. "Isn't that great?"

"It's more than just great," GiGi said. "It's *awesome*."

Georgie and GiGi asked Amy if she liked skateboarding. She said she much preferred roller skating, and told them she had a couple of extra pairs of roller skates that should fit them just fine. Soon the first daughter and the two G's—along with Amy's Secret Service detail—were skating down Pennsylvania Avenue.

Suddenly, and unexpectedly, Georgie and GiGi's roller skates turned into the magical skateboard. And they were off!

The two G's landed at a Habitat for Humanity construction site in Georgia. They were back in the present day.

An elderly man they recognized as Jimmy Carter approached them with a smile. "Hi there, children, I'm glad you came to help."

The former president explained that while Georgie and GiGi were a little too young to be wielding hammers and saws, their help was still very much needed. He handed them bright-yellow hard hats and led them to a tent, where Rosalynn was fixing lunch for the construction crew. Peanut butter and jelly sandwiches were being prepared in an assembly line.

Georgie and GiGi, proudly wearing their hard hats, helped Mrs. Carter assemble the sandwiches. She even taught them the secret to a perfect PB&J— *lots* of peanut butter.

Ronald Reagan

Georgie and GiGi found themselves rolling down a hallway of what appeared to be a hospital.

A security guard reprimanded them, "No skateboarding in the hospital, kids."

The two G's apologized and immediately hopped off the board.

"What do you think we're doing in a *hospital*?" asked Georgie.

"I don't know," GiGi replied. "I've only been to a hospital once before, when I was really young, for a tonsillectomy."

"What's that?"

"It's when you have your tonsils taken out."

"Did it hurt?" asked Georgie, crinkling up his face.

"Not really," GiGi replied, "and I could have as much ice cream as I wanted for a whole week!"

As they approached the nurse's station, there was a song playing softly on the radio about a man eating cars and bars and guitars. They'd never heard a song like that before, but they liked listening to it. It sounded strange but cool.

"Excuse me," GiGi asked a nurse politely. "This may sound like a strange question, but can you tell us what year it is?"

"Very funny," the nurse smirked. "You kids know as well as I do that it's 1981."

They said thank you and scurried off. "Oh I know where we are!" exclaimed Georgie. "We learned in history class that somebody tried to assassinate President Ronald Reagan in 1981 shortly after he took office. Remember?"

"Yah," GiGi replied, "but he was okay, unlike poor Lincoln. And poor JFK. Oh, they were both so nice."

They spotted a lady who they both recognized from the postage stamp as First Lady Nancy Reagan. She was surrounded by Secret Service agents, and she was...laughing! Mrs. Reagan must have already received the news that her husband was going to be just fine.

The children approached and told her they wished the president a speedy recovery.

"Would you kids like to tell him yourselves?" she asked. "Ronnie would love the company from two little rays of sunshine! And everybody else around here is so *old*." Mrs. Reagan then led the two G's into her husband's hospital room.

The kids knew that the 40th president had been a movie star before he was elected governor of California and then president of the United States. They had even watched one of Reagan's best-loved movies, called *Bedtime for Bonzo*, about a professor who takes a chimpanzee home and tries to train it. Marie knew all about old movies, and she guessed that Georgie and GiGi would like that one. And they did! The three of them laughed so hard they almost fell off the couch.

Even though he was older and now lying in a hospital bed, Reagan still looked very much like the young actor they remembered from the movie. And his hair was still pitch-black!

Reagan possessed that 'movie star' quality, and his eyes sparkled as he was introduced to Georgie and GiGi. He had a great sense of humor, too.

"I'll give you two a couple of jokes that you missed," said Mrs. Reagan. "When I got to the hospital, just after Ronnie was shot, he told me, 'Honey, I forgot to duck.' And when a team of doctors were brought in to operate on him, Ronnie—who's a Republican, you know—looked up and said 'I hope you're all Republicans.'"

Mrs. Reagan pecked her husband on the forehead and told him she'd be back in a little while to check on him. "I leave you in good hands," she said with a wink.

"Georgie and GiGi—those sure are nice names," Reagan murmured, still feeling weak. "I've got four kids of my own: Michael, Maureen, Patti and Ron, Jr."

The two G's offered to play with Reagan's kids. They could even teach them skateboarding tricks.

"Well, that's very nice of you, but they're a little older than you two," he told them.

Georgie and GiGi excused themselves for a moment and stepped outside. Whispering, so that no one could overhear them, they decided to help Reagan's speedy recovery by telling him a secret. They would reveal to him that he would become so popular that he would win reelection in 1984 in a landslide. (49 states!)

But when they returned to Reagan's side, he said he was feeling tired and wanted to take a nap.

"I know the feeling, Mr. President," GiGi told him. "After I had my tonsils taken out, I felt like taking naps all the time."

Reagan closed his eyes but continued talking to them.

"Coming so close to death makes me feel I should do whatever I can in the years God has given me to keep the American people out of war and to fight the scourge of Communism; maybe that's the reason I am still alive."

Indeed, Reagan would become well known for championing democracy and fighting against Communism during his presidency. History would recognize his efforts to bring an end to the Cold War between the United States and the Soviet Union and to reduce the threat of nuclear war.

"Are you mad at the guy who shot you?" Georgie asked.

"Well, yes," Reagan said softly. "But I forgive him."

"You do?" asked GiGi. "Does that mean you don't want him to go to jail?"

Reagan opened one eye and looked at her. "Young lady, I may be a forgiving man, but I'm not a fool. Besides, actions have consequences. If you do something wrong, you may be forgiven. But you still have to take responsibility for your actions."

As Reagan drifted into a deep sleep, he dreamt of putting his hand on his heart and watching the American flag blowing mightily against a clear blue sky. Then, in the distance, he saw what looked like two kids gliding through the clouds…on a *skateboard*?

Barack Obama

To meet President Barack Obama, Georgie and GiGi traveled all the way back to 1972, to meet him as a fellow ten-year-old. The magic skateboard brought them to a skate park in Hawaii, where Obama lived for a time when he was a kid.

Georgie and GiGi had never seen palm trees in person, so they were in awe as they looked up and watched them sway. A boy on a skateboard glided up to them and kicked up his board. "Hey there," he said, beaming a bright smile. "I haven't seen you around here. Are you new?"

"It's a long story, but sure, I guess you could say we're new," Georgie said.

"Cool," the boy replied. "I'm Barack, but everybody calls me Barry."

Georgie and GiGi glanced at each other.

"Oh, cool, well I'm George—but everybody calls me Georgie—and this is my friend GiGi. Your last name wouldn't happen to be *Obama*, would it?"

"It is! How did you know?"

"Wild guess?" shrugged Georgie.

Georgie and GiGi were tempted to tell their new friend, Barry, that when he grew up, he would become the President of the United States! But they decided not to spoil the surprise.

Georgie couldn't help but smile to himself, thinking about the YouTube video his father had shown him of President Obama riding a skateboard into a 2012 global summit. When Georgie's Dad told him the video wasn't real—no, Obama did not in fact roll into the summit on a skateboard—Georgie was disappointed. But when he found out that a clip from the made-up moment was awarded GIF of the Year, he cheered up.

After an afternoon of skateboarding, Georgie, GiGi and Barry treated themselves to shaved ices. The crumpled one-dollar bills that Georgie had in one of his cargo pockets were a lot more valuable in 1972 than they were in the present day.

GiGi's favorite flavor was cherry, so her shaved ice was a bright red. Georgie loved coconut, so his was white. Barry picked the flavor called "Razzmaspazz"—so his was blue!

After enjoying their patriotic ices in red, white and blue, the kids were back on their boards. Barry told his new friends that he would teach them how to surf. But he never got the chance.

In a flash, Georgie and GiGi were flying again, soon descending upon Grant Park in the city of Chicago. It was November 4, 2008, and Barrack Obama had just been elected the 44th president of the United States.

More than two hundred thousand people were there. Many of them were clapping and whooping at the top of their lungs. Some had tears streaming down their faces.

It was a historic night. America had just elected its first Black president. Georgie and GiGi could not believe that they were getting to witness *in person* this historic moment, one they'd only read about.

Obama was at the microphone waving and beaming that same bright smile he had as a kid. His wife Michelle and their daughters, Sasha and Malia, were at his side.

> *If there is anyone out there who still doubts that America is a place where all things are possible; who still wonders if the dream of our founders is alive in our time; who still questions the power of our democracy, tonight is your answer.*

"HOPE is that stubborn thing inside us that insists... that something better awaits us so long as we have the courage to keep reaching, to keep working, to keep fighting."

BARACK OBAMA

"Oh, I'm so proud of Barry," GiGi said to Georgie.

"Yeah, and I thought getting elected class president of the fourth grade was a big deal," Georgie replied.

> *It's been a long time coming, but tonight, because of what we did on this day, in this election, at this defining moment, change has come to America.*

There were so many flashes going off from so many camera phones (even flip phones!) that Georgie and GiGi found themselves squinting.

> *As Lincoln said to a nation far more divided than ours, "We are not enemies, but friends... Though passion may have strained, it must not break our bonds of affection." And, to those Americans whose support I have yet to earn, I may not have won your vote, but I hear your voices, I need your help, and I will be your president, too.*

Georgie rubbed his eyes. When he opened them, he saw a young couple that he recognized among the crowd. It was his parents, Cecile and John! Georgie remembered the story of how his parents met—standing in line at the polls on election day in 2008. He figured they must have decided to go and see the president-elect speak. This was their first date!

He thought about pointing out his young parents, who were *on a date*, to GiGi. But for some reason, he decided not to. *Awkward.*

> *For that is the true genius of America—that America can change. Our union can be perfected. And what we have already achieved gives us hope for what we can and must achieve tomorrow.*

Georgie and GiGi found themselves caught up in the moment, and joined the crowd as it chanted *Yes, we can! Yes, we can!*
Wow, they thought, politics is fun!

> *This is our moment. This is our time—to put our people back to work and open doors of opportunity for our kids; to restore prosperity and promote the cause of peace; to reclaim the American Dream and reaffirm that fundamental truth that out of many, we are one; that while we breathe, we hope, and where we are met with cynicism, and doubt, and those who tell us that we can't, we will respond with that timeless creed that sums up the spirit of a people: Yes, we can.*

JOE # KAMALA

JOE BIDEN
The 46th President, 2021–

KAMALA HARRIS
The 49th Vice President, 2021–

Joe Biden
featuring Kamala Harris

The next time Georgie and GiGi got to meet the president, it wasn't part of their summertime skateboard adventure. They were now officially fifth-graders. And their class field trip would be to a place they had already visited (a few times)—the White House!

In the middle of this White House tour, the guide informed their class that President Biden and Vice President Harris would like to take some time out of their day to meet the children.

Soon after, the 46th president, Joe Biden, walked in with his vice president, Kamala Harris, by his side. Georgie and GiGi and their classmates could barely contain their excitement. Even their teachers were excited.

"Hello there, children" President Biden said warmly. "Hi, everybody!" added Vice President Harris, waving both her hands in the air.

The president and vice president were very friendly and offered to answer any questions the children had. One of Georgie and GiGi's classmates asked Biden if he liked being president or vice president better.

The president answered, "Look, I served as vice president in the Obama administration with my good friend Barack. And we made a lot of progress in those eight years. But here's the deal, it's not about looking back at what's behind you. It's about looking ahead at what's in front of you. And folks, we've got a lot of work to do, because there's a lot at stake—nothing less than the very soul of a nation, *our* nation. So that's why, as president, I keep fighting. For your generation, and the one after that, and so on. That's the work of the Biden administration."

"The Biden-*Harris* administration," the vice president chimed in.

One of Georgie and GiGi's classmates then asked Harris what it felt like to be the first female vice president.

"It feels great!" she said with a laugh. "But, honestly, I may be the first woman in this office, but I will certainly not be the last. And you know, we have still not had a woman *president* in this country."

"Not yet!" added Biden.

Then the children were treated to short one-on-ones with the president and vice president, where they got to personally meet them and have their picture taken with them.

Georgie and GiGi asked their teacher if they could ask to meet the president and vice president together and have double the amount of time with them. Their teacher said okay.

After posing for a picture with President Biden and Vice President Harris, Georgie and GiGi told them that they probably knew a lot more about presidential history than typical kids. Biden and Harris seemed delighted to hear this and encouraged them to share their knowledge.

The two G's proceeded to tell them that George Washington was all about truth. Lincoln taught them that freedom and equality were worth fighting for. And Theodore Roosevelt showed them how important it was to protect and conserve the country's natural resources.

"The 'teddy bear' was named after him!" exclaimed GiGi. Both Biden and Harris chuckled.

They continued. FDR emboldened them to be fearless, especially when doing the right thing. JFK led by example; being brave and kind were cool!

And LBJ schooled them on the terrible nature of discrimination and prejudice.

They even learned from Nixon that haters only end up destroying themselves. "He's really not a very good singer," Georgie added. Biden and Harris didn't quite know what to make of that one.

"And we learned that even though Andrew Johnson, and Bill Clinton, and Donald Trump were officially impeached, they were all allowed to stay on as president, because—"

Georgie and GiGi sang, "The House voted to indict, but the Senate said no, it's alright!"

"Oh, that's clever, children!" said Harris.

From Carter they learned how important it is to help people. And from Reagan they learned how important it is to forgive people.

Obama, in addition to being really good on a skateboard, helped them realize that with hope, anything is possible—especially in America.

President Biden and Vice President Harris were dazzled by how knowledgeable Georgie and GiGi seemed to be about presidential history.

"You know, Kamala," Biden said, "We may just have a future president and vice president on our hands here."

"Yah," giggled GiGi, "Georgie would make a great vice president."

At the skate park later that night, Georgie and GiGi were still on cloud nine. Not only had they gotten the chance to visit the White House (again), but they had also impressed the president and vice president of the United States!

"And we only shared with them *some* of what we learned!" boasted Georgie. "Hey, G," he continued. "Can you give me a push? It feels like one of my wheels is stuck."

"Sure, G," she answered.

GiGi hopped off her board and gave Georgie a soft push. And just like that, they were flying.

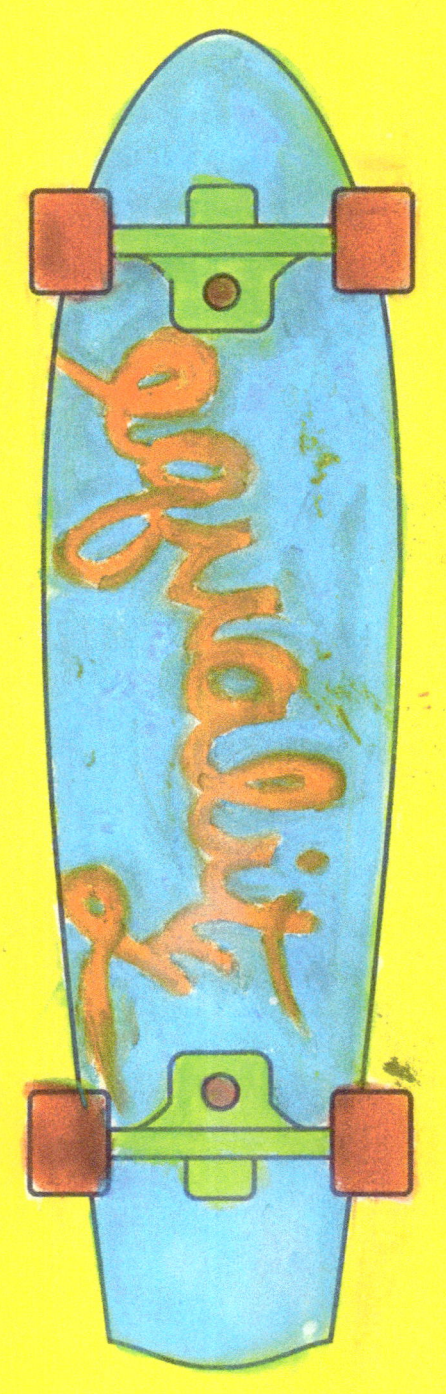

AFTERWORD

Hey kids! If you are reading this it means you got to the end of the book! Or at least you paged through the book to look at The Artist CLEO's Skateboard Gallery, which is pretty cool.

I hope you had as much fun reading this book as I had writing it. I'm so glad I got to introduce you to Georgie and GiGi. Georgie is based on me as a kid, but he is probably a lot more fun than I was. GiGi is inspired by my coolest family and friends and most of all by The Artist CLEO. Like CLEO, GiGi is super athletic. And just as CLEO does it all—from skateboarding to drawing to playing the cello—so does GiGi!

I love the idea of making Georgie and GiGi skateboarders who could time travel on an extra wide bright red skateboard. Fun fact: Just as GiGi decorated her board with stickers, so too did CLEO decorate our skateboards.

The most exciting part of their being able to time travel was how Georgie and GiGi got to meet past presidents and learn about how important character is for all people, especially leaders.

And that is the point of the book, to help young readers like you (all readers really!) remember how important it is to want our leaders to be good people. What is more important than being a good person? What is more important than knowing the difference between right and wrong? And what's more important than having the guts to do the right thing, even if it may not be the easiest or most popular thing.

We want that in our friends and families, our Girl Scout and Boy Scout leaders, our teachers, firemen, police, and of course, in our presidents. Right?!

To me, the best people speak from the heart, tell it like it is, and always strive to make the right decision, no matter what. That takes guts.

Having character and having guts go hand in hand. For example, if someone in your class is being mean, are you courageous enough to call him or her out in front of everyone? When I was growing up, sometimes I had the guts to do the right thing, and sometimes I didn't. Looking back, I can tell you that those decisions stay with you.

And today, when I have to find it in me to do the right thing, I lean on all of my experiences going back to when I was your age to be courageous.

The other point of this book is to see how Georgie and GiGi not only witness history, but also participate in making history. They help Abraham Lincoln write the historic Gettysburg Address. They even help George Washington cross the Delaware River to defeat the British. (That's my favorite chapter, but then George Washington is my *fave prez*!)

They're *gutsy* kids!

My hope is that by showing how Georgie and GiGi work alongside the presidents throughout moments in history, we see the good in our leaders—and in ourselves.

Trying to be a good person and having the guts to do the right thing is important for all of us. And when we see that in a president, it's special.

I'm writing this just a few days after Donald Trump defeated Kamala Harris in the 2024 presidential election. Cards on the table, I was for Vice President Harris. So, in the aftermath of the election, my thoughts are tumbling through my brain like a baseball cap in the clothes drier.

But as Thomas Jefferson said:

*We in America do not have government by the majority.
We have government by the majority who participate.*

Democracy worked even if I do not agree with the outcome.

Trump's win for the presidency in both 2016 and 2024 reflects another Jeffersonian nugget of wisdom, namely that "a little rebellion now and then is a good thing."

He was not talking about a rebellion as fighting and violence. He meant that shaking things up every now and the is "as necessary in the political world as storms are in the physical."

In conclusion, win or lose, let us pick ourselves up, hold our heads high, with the wisdom to know what is good and right, and the courage – or guts! – to fight for it. That (and voting, when you are all old enough) is our superpower!

George S. Corey
Washington, D.C.
November 12, 2024

ACKNOWLEDGMENTS

I would like to thank my young readers and fans of Georgie and GiGi. I am especially grateful to those young readers who are related to me, my 14 nieces and nephews. Their youthful wisdom and enthusiasm continue to inspire me. I am also grateful to the entire team at Cinergistik, and to everyone who lent their talents to bringing this story to life, in all its forms: hardcover, digital, audio, and now paperback. I am most thankful to my wife Cynthia, my entire family, and all my friends for their feedback and support. Finally, the magnificent artwork by the extraordinary artist CLEO makes *Presidential Conversations for Kids* come alive on the page as well as in life.

ABOUT THE AUTHOR

George S. Corey is an attorney and lifelong student of history. He is the author of the acclaimed books *Presidential Conversations* and *Presidential Conversations for Kids*. George is co-creator, along with The Artist CLEO, of the award-winning podcast *The Social Contract*, now in its third season and available on all major podcast platforms. He lives in Washington, D.C. with his wife Cynthia, also an attorney.

www.georgescorey.com

ABOUT THE ARTIST

The Artist CLEO is an acclaimed visual artist who creates in multiple mediums. Along with author George S. Corey she is co-creator of the award-winning podcast *The Social Contract*, now in its third season. A frequent collaborator with George, CLEO's socially conscious art can be seen in the books *Presidential Conversations* and *Presidential Conversations for Kids* ("history with a wink"- Kirkus Reviews). She remains committed to inspiring young minds and nurturing tomorrow's leaders.

www.theartistcleo.com

Learn more about the award-winning
podcast The Social Contract:

www.myTSCpodcast.com

www.ingramcontent.com/pod-product-compliance
Lightning Source LLC
Chambersburg PA
CBHW040852260125
20855CB00022B/1843